Sydney Learns to Share

Based on the Bible verse: "Store up for yourselves treasures in heaven." (Matthew 6:20, NIV)

by Paula J. Bussard

Illustrated by Lawrence Goodridge

S0-BYB-726

Copyright © 1985, Christine Wyrtzen Ministry.
Published by The STANDARD PUBLISHING Company, Cincinnati, Ohio.
Printed in U.S.A.   3381

The sunshine warmed the trees one crisp fall morning in Critter County.

Sydney woke up early and began to plan his day.

"First," he thought, "I'll fix my favorite breakfast—an acorn omelet with maple syrup on the side. Then I will continue my search for nuts to store for the winter. I can't think of anything I would rather do than collect nuts so I will have plenty to eat all winter."

So after he cleaned his breakfast dishes, he got his bag out of the closet.

"This should be full by dinner time tonight," he thought.

Just as he was reaching for his favorite orange jacket, the phone rang.

"Hello, Sydney, this is Kandy," the voice said. "My cousin, Katy, is visiting me, and her car won't start. Could you find time to come over and try to fix it?"

"No, I can't. I have to collect nuts so I will have plenty to eat this winter," said Sydney.

"Oh, Sydney, you have weeks of nice weather to collect your nuts. Please come," pleaded Kandy.

But Sydney would not come.

So Kandy hung up the phone and was very sad. She thought Sydney would rather fill his shelves with food than help his friends.

Later that morning, as Sydney was passing the Critter County Nursery, the skunk family was beginning to take a walk.

"Good morning, Sydney," said the daddy skunk. "Would you like to join our little family walk? We could use some help. My wife is so tired because she was up all night with the babies. It seems they have learned how to turn on their smells. Everyone was complaining!"

"No, I can't help. I must collect nuts!" explained Sydney. "I want to have plenty so I will stay full all winter."

"Well, OK," said Mrs. Skunk, sadly, "but we could use your help."

Many days passed. All the red, orange, and yellow leaves began to fall from the trees. Every day, some critters would ask Sydney to come over to eat or play. He would always say his grocery shopping was more important.

This made the other animals very sad.
Whenever one of the animals would tell
Sydney that he spent too much time filling
his closet and not enough time with his
friends, Sydney would say,
"But there's nothing wrong with collecting
nuts. I need them to eat."

The days passed, and soon a blanket of fluffy white snow covered all of Critter County. The animals had so much fun building snow sculptures and igloos. They loved to make each letter of the alphabet out of snow.

One morning while some of the critters were having a contest to see who could build the very best sculpture, Sydney became very sick. He was in his tree house, and he couldn't get out of bed! His fever was 104°, and his tummy really hurt!

"I need to call my friends to come and help me," he thought.

He finally got enough strength to crawl over to his window.

"Help! Somebody help me! I've got a bad bug," he called. "Oh, excuse me, ants and grasshoppers. I mean I am sick!! Can somebody come to help me, *please?*"

When all of the animals heard Sydney's
call for help, they remembered how many
times they had asked him for help, but he
had been too busy.

They all gathered in a circle.
"Sydney was as busy as a bee when I
needed help with the honey last summer,"
buzzed Queen Bee. "He wouldn't help me!"

"To have a friend, you must be a friend,"
said Kandy, the kangaroo.

"Yeah," said Mrs. Skunk. "This whole
situation smells pretty bad, if you ask me."
"You should know," said Poncho Pig.

About that time, one of the Cool Cats decided to speak up for what is right.

"My friends and neighbors ... let us remember to love one another. We need to pitch in and help Sydney. Then he will learn what friendship is all about."

"You are absolutely right. I am going to rush home and fix him some walnut soup," offered Kandy with a sweet smile on her face.

"If someone will carry me up to his tree house, I'll stay beside his bed," said Thomas T. Turtle. "If he needs a footstool to get up or down, he can step on my back."

All the other animals began making plans
to help Sydney. Even Lenny, the lion,
climbed into bed with him to cover him
with his mane so the sick little squirrel would
stay warm.

The next day, all of Sydney's friends came to his house to help some more. They were so surprised to find Sydney up and around!

"Thank you, my dear friends. Your love and attention made me recover very quickly," said Sydney. "My tummy and head feel great today, and my heart feels even better because it is filled with love for you."

"You have taught me there is something more important than having food, toys, and a nice house. You have taught me that it is more important to share with my friends," said Sydney. "The Bible teaches, 'Store up for yourselves treasures in heaven.' You are my treasures!"

"All of you are invited to my house for an acorn roast and peanut brittle ice cream," Sydney continued. "Come on up and share everything in my house."

Friends are so very important to us. I am so glad that you are my friend. Would you do something for your ol' friend, Sydney?

Would you look through all your toys, books, and clothes until you find something that you can give away ... something that will make someone else happy. Be sure Mommy says it is OK. Then give it away! You will be learning what it means in Matthew 6:20, when it says, "Store up for yourselves treasures in heaven."

Then write to me in Critter County to tell me what you gave away and what your friend said. Sharing ... that is what friends are to do!

Write to   Sydney
Box 8
Critter County
Loveland, Ohio 45140

The Christine Wyrtzen Critter County album is available in its entirety from your local Christian bookstore or Standard Publishing.